# THE BRAVEST MAN IN THE WORLD

# THE BRAVEST MAN IN THE WORLD

# PATRICIA POLACCO

A Paula Wiseman Book
SIMON & SCHUSTER BOOKS FOR YOUNG READERS
New York  London  Toronto  Sydney  New Delhi

To those lost on the *Titanic* and to their families

SIMON & SCHUSTER BOOKS FOR YOUNG READERS
An imprint of Simon & Schuster Children's Publishing Division
1230 Avenue of the Americas, New York, New York 10020
Copyright © 2019 by Patricia Polacco
All rights reserved, including the right of reproduction in whole or in part in any form.
SIMON & SCHUSTER BOOKS FOR YOUNG READERS is a trademark of Simon & Schuster, Inc.
For information about special discounts for bulk purchases, please contact Simon & Schuster Special Sales
at 1-866-506-1949 or business@simonandschuster.com.
The Simon & Schuster Speakers Bureau can bring authors to your live event. For more information or to book an event,
contact the Simon & Schuster Speakers Bureau at 1-866-248-3049 or visit our website at www.simonspeakers.com.
Book design by Laurent Linn
The text for this book was set in Chaparrel Pro.
The illustrations for this book were rendered in two and six B pencils and acetone markers.
Manufactured in China
0719 SCP
First Edition
2 4 6 8 10 9 7 5 3 1
Library of Congress Cataloging-in-Publication Data
Names: Polacco, Patricia, author, illustrator.
Title: The bravest man in the world / Patricia Polacco.
Description: First edition. | New York : Simon & Schuster Books for Young Readers, [2019] | "A Paula Wiseman Book." |
Summary: In 1912, orphaned Irish street musician Jonathan Harker accidentally stows away on the Titanic, where he is
befriended by Wallace Hartley, called "the bravest man in the world" for playing violin with the band as the Titanic sank.
Includes historical note.
Identifiers: LCCN 2018016740 | ISBN 9781481494618 (hardcover) | ISBN 9781481494625 (e-book)
Subjects: LCSH: Hartley, Wallace, 1878-1912—Juvenile fiction. | CYAC: Hartley, Wallace, 1878-1912—Fiction. |
Violin—Fiction. | Music—Fiction. | Orphans—Fiction. | Stowaways—Fiction. | Shipwrecks—Fiction. |
Titanic (Steamship)—Fiction.
Classification: LCC PZ7.P75186 Br 2019 | DDC [Fic]—dc23 LC record available at https://lccn.loc.gov/2018016740

There were exactly two things that Jonathan Harker Weeks didn't like—the taste of liver, and having to practice piano.

"Grandfather . . . why do I have to practice? Pleeeeeease let me go out and play stickball with Joey and Nathan . . . while it's still light out," he pleaded.

"I promise you, Jonathan," his grandfather insisted, "you'll never regret studying your music. It will bring you endless joy someday."

"Joy!" Jonathan hissed. "This is sissy stuff. I don't want to be a sissy."

"And I suppose that means that you think I wasted thirty years of my life playing first-chair violin with the philharmonic?" Grandfather thundered.

Jonathan dropped his head. "What I meant to say was that I want to be a superhero . . . strong and brave . . . ," he muttered.

"Jonathan, come over here. I have a story to tell you," Grandfather announced as he patted the footstool by his chair. "Come, sit!" he invited.

"Did I ever tell you that I once knew the bravest man in the world?" Grandfather trumpeted.

"In the *whole* world?" Jonathan asked as he took his seat on the footstool.

"In the *whole world*!" his grandfather echoed as he got a faraway look in his eyes.

"Where? . . . How?" Jonathan asked, and he drew close to his grandfather.

*First of all, I need to tell you that the woman I have referred to all these many years as me mum* wasn't my mother at all. Margaret Weeks took me in when I was nine years old. I wasn't born here in New York, as you have believed. I was actually born in the slums of Ireland . . . Queenstown, more than seventy-nine years ago. I never knew my father, and me mum and I lived in a humble room in the house. But I knew that me mum loved me and that she was battling to provide what she could for us both.

We lived very near the shipyards and harbor. She cleaned houses and took in laundry. Even in the face of this poverty, she managed to buy me a fiddle. She even saw to it that a street busker down the hall taught me to play it. After a time I was able to earn money for us by playing on the streets with other musicians and sprookers. At the end of the day, me mum made us warm soup and held me close and told me that someday I'd be a fine gentleman and would play for the king!

The winter after my eighth birthday, me mum died of quick consumption.

I had no choice. I took my fiddle and ran to the shipyard and played on the docks.

I slept where I could, ate when I had enough money to buy a meal. I was always looking over my shoulder because others told me that Darby Hooks and his two toadies were looking for me.

Sure enough, one day they spotted me. I had set up right next to the docks, and it was late at night. A steamship was going to put in at eleven or so and would be carrying rich passengers that might throw coins to me while I played on the mooring.

"I'll have your guts for garters!" I heard the familiar voice call out. It was Darby. He and his thugs lunged at me. Darby emptied my case of its money, then seized me by the neck and lifted me clean off my feet. One of his toadies picked up my fiddle and handed it to Darby, who crushed it into a thousand pieces in front of my face. Then I heard a bobby's whistle. "Coppers," one of the thugs crowed. Darby dropped me, and I wriggled away and ran for my life.

I found myself in one of the warehouses where the bags of mail were waiting to be picked up. Then I heard Darby rumble in behind me. I dropped to my hands and knees and crawled into a large bag full of letters and hid. I tried to be completely still so that no one would find me. Especially Darby. I could hear the voices of the men loading the bags onto carts. I decided to stay put until they were gone. As I lay there in the darkness, I started to cry. All I could think of was how hard me mum had worked so that I could have that fiddle, and how those terrible men had broken it and my dreams.

I don't know how long I was in the mailbag, but the next thing I remember was a rude awakening as the bag dropped to the floor with a thud. I could hear voices talking around me again. I didn't dare call out, so I just stayed as still as I could until the voices were gone.

Then I crawled out and made a run for it. I darted down what seemed to be endless halls. There were many doorways that had numbers on them. Was I in a hotel? Just then I heard voices behind me, and I dodged into a room that had the door ajar.

It was at that moment that I eyed the most beautiful fiddle, in a fine leather valise resting on a bunk. There were uniforms hanging in the wardrobe. They were elegant and snappy. I couldn't help myself. I took a seat and picked up the fiddle and started to play.

Tears rolled down my cheeks. My heart flooded with memories of me mum, and I cried bitterly.

"Well, well, laddie," a voice called from behind me. I caught my breath. A tall man was standing there in the doorway. I was waiting for him to scream at me the way most adults did. But he was calm and gentle.

"I must say, I have never seen anyone play the violin holding it just so," he said as he drew closer.

"It's—it's the way I learnt it," I stammered.

"The bow. . . . You are bowing the violin backward. . . . Did you know that?" he said with a warm smile.

I didn't know if I should run for it, or stay.

The young man gently took the violin from me and placed it under his chin and began to play . . . just for me.

I had never heard a sound so sweet. I swayed with each sweep of his bow. I watched his fingers dance over the strings. I was fascinated by how he was holding the fiddle—under his chin! And he was pulling the bow across the strings in the direction opposite from how I did. Then I tried.

"Well, I should say, you'll be playing for the White Star Line sooner than you think . . . and the lads and I will be put out of a job." He laughed.

I smiled, but I didn't know what a white star line was.

"And what's your name, laddie?" he asked.

Just then there was a light rapping on the door. A rosy-cheeked stout woman with a tray brimming with sandwiches and tea trundled in.

"Mr. Hartley, dear . . . thought you might be wanting a little something before your midnight performance." She set the tray down.

I was so hungry that I couldn't take my eyes off the tray.

"And who might this little chappy be, Mr. Hartley?" she chirped as she poured the tea. Mr. Hartley looked at me and smiled.

"Jonathan. . . . Jonathan Harker," I said quietly.

"And how would you be knowin' Mr. Hartley here?" she inquired as she gave me a wink.

"I found him playing my violin, Mrs. Weeks," Mr. Hartley said softly, smiling at me.

I started to cry.

"Darlin' boy . . . it can't be as bad as all that!" Mrs. Weeks cooed and hugged me close.

"If you are lost on this ship," Mr. Hartley said quietly, "we'll help you find your family. Where are they? In third class . . . steerage?"

"Ship!" I exclaimed as I reeled backward. "I'm on a ship?"

"Darlin' boy, you're on the ship of dreams . . . the grandest, fastest, and largest ocean liner in the world. We're bound for America!" Mrs. Weeks sang out.

I lost my footing and sat down in a heap.

"I ain't supposed to be on a ship. . . . I was hiding. That's the last thing I remember," I muttered.

"My poor lamb." Mrs. Weeks hummed as she rocked me in her arms.

"Looks like our little chappy is a stowaway," Mr. Hartley said thoughtfully.

"There would be no point in notifying the purser or the captain. The ship is too far under way to turn back," Mrs. Weeks whispered as she looked pleadingly at Mr. Hartley.

"Then we shall have to make the best of it," Mr. Hartley said with resolve.

So Mr. Hartley and Mrs. Weeks agreed to keep me somewhat of a secret.

"You'll be working with me in the galley," Mrs. Weeks told me.

The next morning as I worked folding linens with Mrs. Weeks, I learned that this was to be her last ocean crossing and that she and her husband were settling in a place called Brooklyn. Her husband was already there.

The best part of my day was watching Mr. Hartley and the other musicians play in the dining room.

"Please, Mr. Hartley, can you show me how you and the others do it? . . . I want to play as wonderfully as you do!" I pleaded after his shift was over.

"Well, can you read music, lad?" he asked me as he drew up a stand in front of us.

I looked confused. "I learned my pieces by memorizing them from the man who taught me," I muttered.

"I know most of what I play by heart as well," Mr. Hartley replied, "but all of us follow the music so that we play together and in harmony with one another. Watch now as I start to play. You'll notice that when the music goes up in scale, the notes climb higher on those lines on the page. . . . Watch now," he said as he began to play.

Sure enough, as he played, I followed the notes as his fingers moved up and down the neck. "The vertical lines determine the phrasing and how fast you play the piece," he added.

I watched his fingers intently.

"Mr. Hartley, sir, can you teach me how to do this?" I asked shyly as we walked on the promenade deck.

"Well, laddie, we have only a few more days on this vessel, but I'll show you what I can."

About then some of the other musicians came by.

"May I present Master Jonathan Harker, a street musician from Queenstown," Mr. Hartley announced.

Each one of them played a small ditty on their instrument and bowed.

Then they all rushed off to play for luncheon.

"Here you are, lad. This is an extra violin that we keep. Why don't you take it for as long as you are on this ship, and practice . . . practice . . . practice," Mr. Hartley said, and then he left, smiling broadly.

As I was playing, an older boy came onto the promenade deck. Then he offered me his hand. "Everyone calls me Dub."

I liked him straightaway!

"So are you one of the musicians for the White Star Line?" he asked.

"No. Mr. Hartley has been giving me lessons. I've been paying my fiddle in Queenstown. You know, street sprookin'," I answered.

"Thought you was too young to be part of that lot," he said, and he smiled. "I'm headin' up to third class to play with the lads. You want in with us?" Dub invited.

I nodded enthusiastically, and we tore up the halls and stairs and spilled out onto the deck marked THIRD CLASS.

The next day, I heard Mr. Hartley call out to me from the forward deck. "Jonathan, I have some time. Let me hear what you have practiced today." Then he motioned for me to come to him.

I had been practicing almost every waking hour that I could. I was anxious to see what Mr. Hartley would think.

After I played for Mr. Hartley, he announced that he knew how much I had been practicing and that he had a surprise for me. "I have taken the liberty of arranging a meeting with Mr. John Jacob Astor for him to hear you play!"

I must have looked puzzled.

"Jonathan, he's one of the richest and most influential men in New York City. He supports the arts. He has direct connections with the Institute of Musical Art," Mr. Hartley crowed as he all but danced around the room.

"And if he likes what he hears—and I know he will—and believes in you just as I do . . . my boy, the sky is the limit!"

"What do you mean, Mr. Hartley?" I asked.

"My boy, one word from him, and you will have a place at the institute. You'll be set for life. You'll become a very, very fine musician!" Mr. Hartley told me.

About then Mrs. Weeks poked her head into the room. "Get a move on, my dear boy. We have to set up the dining room for luncheon," she called out, and then bustled down the hall.

I told her all about the meeting I would have with Mr. Astor later that day.
"Oh, my dear child," she cooed as she held my face in her hands. "You'll be
rounded with the toffs," she said, and chortled.

"I do believe that you are the luckiest lad in the world," she added. "Just look
at how your fortune has changed in less than a week. To think, you were a street
sprooker in Ireland, homeless and an orphan, and now you are on the most
luxurious ship on the sea, steaming for America!

"And you are going to meet with John Jacob Astor!" she said dreamily.

"Look smart, lad. Here he comes with his party. Look at how they walk and how beautifully dressed they are. You'll be one of them someday," she whispered as she nudged me softly.

After luncheon was over, Mr. Hartley and I were on our way to the stateroom of Mr. Astor. "Now, remember, lad," Mr. Hartley said. "Do not speak unless you are spoken to, and always address the gentlemen as 'sir' and the ladies as 'madam.' Answer them directly and look them directly in their eyes, but most of all, play. Play, dear lad, with all of your heart! You are so talented. Every one of them will see this immediately!"

When Mr. Hartley introduced me to Mr. Astor, I remembered everything he had told me. Finally it was time to play. Mr. Hartley took a seat at the grand piano to accompany me. He had given me his prize violin to play. I raised it to my chin and drew the bow across the strings. I was afraid to look at Mr. Astor and his guests. . . . I just played. I played with all of my soul and thought of me mum and how proud she would have been to see this. I felt tears burning in my eyes and truly felt that she was watching over me.

When we finished our concert, Mr. Astor and the others burst into enthusiastic applause. It was for me! Mr. Hartley excused me from the room and asked me to wait in the hall. I was there for what seemed like the longest time . . . but when he came out, his face was beaming.

"Well, laddie, you did it!" he chirped. "Mr. Astor is sending a message on the ship-to-shore telegraph as we speak, securing you a place at the Institute of Musical Art!"

I was thrilled beyond reason, but where was I going to live? Who would take care of me?

"Am I going to stay with you, Mr. Hartley?" I blurted out.

"Oh, no, laddie. I'm returning to Dewsbury to marry my sweetheart, Maria. Then I'll be taking up a post at the music academy there," he called out. "You'll be staying in New York!"

Later that night as we left Mr. Hartley's cabin, I noticed that his violin was different from all the others. "There's an inscription on it," Mr. Hartley told me. "It's my sweetheart's name—Maria Robinson. She also gave me this fine case. See there? She even had my initials put on it."

Then he whispered, "You've changed your stars this day, lad. This will be a day that you'll remember as long as you live!" Mr. Hartley looked up at the stars.

We went to a party in steerage. Folks were dancing about, whirling, laughing, and singing. There was plenty of grog and food! I sat right down with the other musicians and commenced playing my fiddle.

I hadn't been up that late in a very long time. Doing scullery duties in the dining room made it necessary to rise early, but that night nothing mattered. I felt merry and as light as a feather.

I saw it was close to midnight, nearly April 15, 1912 . . . a date that would live in infamy in my heart for the rest of my life.

The ship lurched and shuddered and rumbled. No one noticed at first . . . but then there was another sharp bump, and the engines stopped. The whole ship was vibrating and shuddering. Then the lights flickered and the shaking got more pronounced. The movement was strong enough that some of those who were walking lost their footing and fell to the deck. Everyone became quiet and stood almost motionless, as if listening for some sort of telling sound. Then someone called out, "This here ship is listing. It's listing to starboard!"

The floor seemed to be tilting more and more by the second. It was even getting hard to stand without hanging on. About then a crewman hurtled down the stairs from the bridge above us. "We've hit an iceberg! This ship has hit a damned iceberg!" he shouted with alarm.

"Iceberg! How could that be? We're too far south to be near them!" an off-duty engine room mate barked.

"Well, we have hit one. Now everyone needs to get to the main deck and report to the purser. He'll know what to do next," the crewman answered.

Everyone bustled about, pulling on their coats and the life preservers being handed out by the crew. "This way, laddie," Mrs. Weeks called out as she pushed through the horrified crowd.

The panic grew. The entire crowd stampeded like frightened cattle on their way to the slaughterhouse. I was run over and pushed to the deck. People were stepping on me in total madness, to make it into the lifeboats on the main deck. Mr. Hartley and Mrs. Weeks found me and held me between them as they pulled me to safety.

On the main deck the crew was trying to maintain order. "Are we going to be all right, Mrs. Weeks?" I asked as I searched her face.

"Of course, my darlin'. Haven't you heard that this ship is *unsinkable*? Nothing on earth could make this one go down," she said with assurance. When I looked at Mr. Hartley's face, he looked very concerned.

Then there was a booming sound, and flares were streaking high up into the night sky. "What are those, Mr. Hartley?" I asked.

"Those are distress signals so that any passing ships can come to our aid. Don't worry, lad. Someone will surely come in time. We're perfectly safe," Mr. Hartley whispered as he tried to smile.

Just then Dub came running up to us. "The whole starboard side is ripped open. The water is pouring into the engine rooms and lower berths," he said with alarm.

"The bulkheads should hold and contain the water so that only the compartments compromised by the torn hull will flood," we heard a crew member say to Dub.

"But that's just it, sir. All of them are failing. We're taking in the sea faster than anyone could have thought," Dub answered.

"We'd better deploy the lifeboats," the purser called out.

"There aren't enough lifeboats to take all of the passengers," Dub muttered.

"How do you know that?" I asked him.

"Me da was one of the shipbuilders in Ireland. He said that they removed half of the lifeboats just before this trip."

I don't think I'll ever forget the look that came over Dub's face at that moment.

About then the purser ordered that the lifeboats be filled and lowered.

"I'm tellin' ya, there ain't enough lifeboats . . . not for this many people!" Dub insisted as he eyed the magnitude of the gathering crowd.

This is when everything seemed to change. There was an air of urgency, and everyone knew on a gut level that we hadn't much time to leave the ship. Men were pushing women and children out of their way and scrambling to get into the boats. Some people were fighting and tugging at life preservers. There weren't enough of those, either.

When the purser drew his pistol and fired into the air, I realized the true gravity of the situation.

"Only women and children are to be loaded into the lifeboats at this time," the purser cried out. "They have priority. . . . ONLY WOMEN AND CHILDREN!"

Mrs. Weeks never lost her grip on me. We were being pushed farther and farther back toward the bulkheads by the panicking throngs.

"Mrs. Weeks, we aren't going to make it. We'll never get on a lifeboat!" I cried.

The purser fired his gun into the air again and again and tried to maintain order. He and many crew members pushed the men back and pulled women with children forward to reach the boats. That's when I saw Mr. Hartley and the others playing their instruments. I broke free of Mrs. Weeks and ran to him and hugged him. "Please, please, Mr. Hartley. Come with us. Please, sir, come with us!" I begged him and cried bitterly. He knelt down next to me and held me.

"No, laddie. I must stay. I must stay and try to soothe these poor souls. Don't you see, lad? They are terrified. My music will help them. It will," he whispered as his eyes filled with tears.

"No . . . no, Mr. Hartley. Then I'm staying with you . . . here!" I cried.

"My dear boy, you have a grand future waiting for you in America. You *must* go. It's written in the stars. Remember?" Mr. Hartley hugged me.

Then I spotted Dub. He was standing next to one of the stairways. He wasn't making a move for the lifeboats. "Dub. . . . Dub. . . . We've got to get onto a lifeboat," I said as I reached for him.

"Old son, I'm nearly fifteen, and I'm a man, I'll be bound. I'm stayin'. . . . I'm staying with all of the other men," he whispered as tears ran down his cheeks.

Just at that moment Mrs. Weeks found me and grabbed me by the hand. "We have to go, my darling. They have room for only a few more on that lifeboat yonder," she said frantically as she gestured to a half-full boat of scared children and sobbing women.

"We can't leave Mr. Hartley. We just can't!" I sobbed as she tried to pull me along.

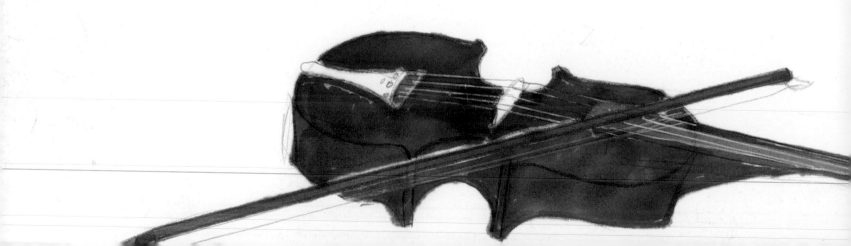

Mr. Hartley hugged us both and knelt again by me.

"Jonathan, behold. This woman is now your mother. Mrs. Weeks and her husband are taking you in. You will dwell in her home and heart. Now you belong to her." Mr. Hartley pushed me into her waiting arms. She hugged and kissed both Mr. Hartley and me. As Mrs. Weeks and I were pushed toward the lifeboat, I reached back and seized his warm hand and cleaved mine to his.

"My darling, my darling," Mrs. Weeks whispered as she rocked me in her arms.

I hung on hard to Mr. Hartley's hand all the way to the edge of the ship, and stayed holding his hand as the purser helped me and Mrs. Weeks into the lifeboat.

As the boat was being lowered by ropes down the side of the ship, I hung on to Mr. Hartley's hand as long as I could. Finally the weight of the boat wrenched my hand from his. He leaned over the side and said one last thing to me.

"Remember, Jonathan . . . every violin has a soul, and it has its own voice. Now go give your violin a voice that comes from your very soul. God bless."

I watched tears fill his eyes and looked into his face as long as I could. Then our lifeboat crashed onto the surface of the mean black waters. Our crewman started rowing. He seemed frantic to get away from the hull of that ship.

I collapsed into Mrs. Weeks's arms and sobbed. Both of us did. How could this be happening? As we got farther and farther away from the ship, it was clear that it was sinking, and sinking fast.

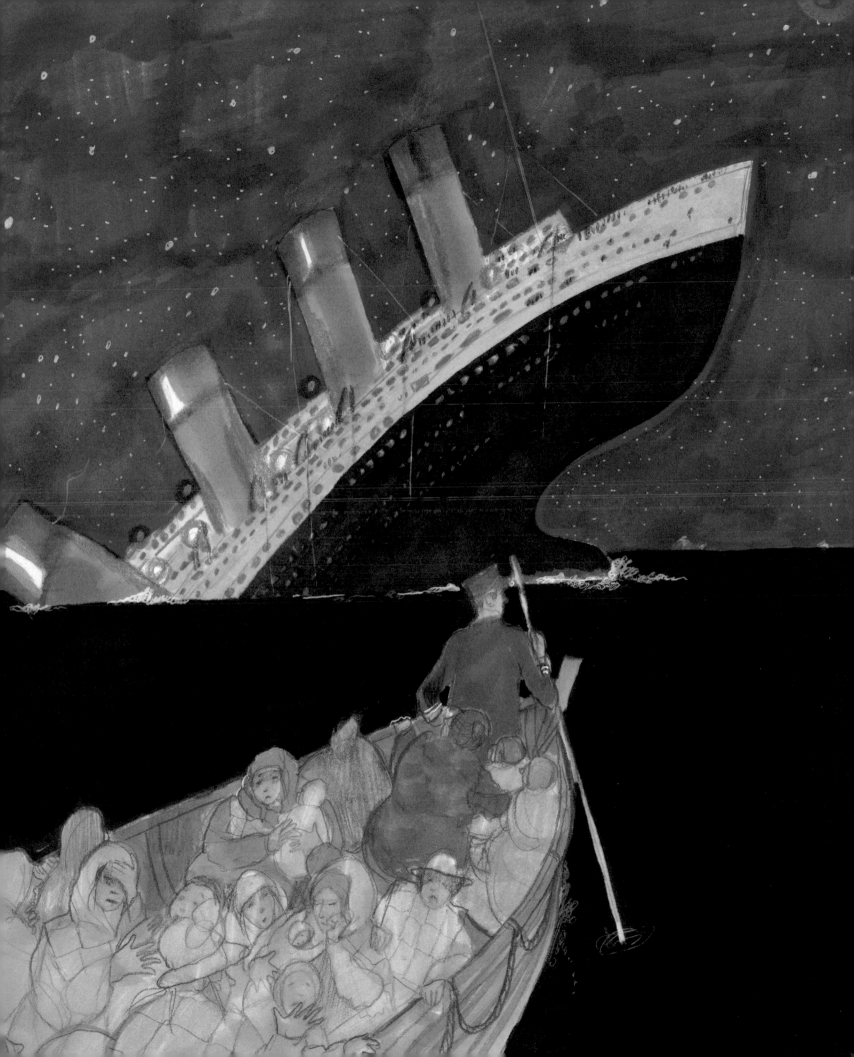

But Mr. Hartley and his musicians were still playing. . . . I could hear the tones of the hymn "Nearer, My God, to Thee." It seemed to calm those who were still clinging to life. Some of the men on the ship burst into the words of the hymn.

That was one of the last sounds that filled my heart that night and brought me any comfort at all.

Then all of us in the lifeboat gasped as the stern of that ship started to sink into the water. That black, cruel, freezing ocean swallowed it up and boiled for a moment with white foam. . . .

Then there was silence. . . .

Twenty lifeboats were in the water. Only seven hundred people made it onto them. Fifteen hundred souls were left on that sinking ship. . . .

Then the bow turned down into the black waters. The stern crashed back down and appeared to be upright. The bow disappeared beneath the surface.

"Now, child, do you understand . . . the bravery of Wallace Hartley?" Grandfather asked Jonathan. "His music was the last thing that those fifteen hundred heard before they sank into a freezing watery grave. That was Mr. Hartley's last magnificent gift to those terrified, frightened people that awful, dreadful night. Mr. Hartley stood there on that deck with freezing numbing water lapping at his ankles and played. . . . *He played with grace . . . grace under fire!*" Jonathan's grandfather started to weep.

"What happened then, Grampa?" Jonathan asked as he took his grandfather's hand.

"The lifeboats were lashed together, and we floated for hours and hours. At first there was crying and sobbing, but after a time that stopped and gave way to an eerie quiet. Everyone just stared into the distance . . . in shock, I presume. But with the breaking of dawn the next morning, the *Carpathia*, a ship that answered our distress calls, arrived and rescued us and lifted us all aboard. That ship brought us here to New York."

"And what about Mr. Hartley?" Jonathan whispered.

"His body wasn't found for two weeks. When it was recovered, it was sent back to England . . . to Dewsbury to Maria Robinson, his fiancée. Wallace Hartley was given a hero's funeral. Most of England—and the world, for that matter—honored him and mourned his loss. All of the newspaper headlines called him THE BRAVEST MAN WHO EVER LIVED . . . and, indeed he was. . . . Indeed he was," Jonathan's grandfather said wistfully.

"Can you imagine the majesty and harrowing strength . . . the limitless bravery in that man's heart, to stand and play on that deck of a doomed ship, knowing that he was about to drown . . ." Jonathan's grandfather's voice trailed off.

"So Mrs. Weeks became your mother, and you went to the Institute of Musical Art just as Mr. Hartley had wished," Jonathan said in quiet wonder.

"And from that time on, every note I played—or ever shall play . . .
there he is also, Jonathan. There he is also. . . .
Wallace Hartley, the Bravest Man in the World."

This story is set in the year 1982, seventy years after the nine-year-old Jonathan was a stowaway aboard the *Titanic*. In 1982 the wreckage at the bottom of the Atlantic had not yet been found.

There are varying accounts of what happened to Wallace Hartley's violin. For many years it was believed that Wallace Hartley's violin went with down the *Titanic*. Some accounts say that the violin was recovered and put in the hold of the *Carpathia* as the people in the lifeboats were rescued. Some accounts say that the valise and violin were found when Wallace Hartley was recovered ten days after the sinking. All accounts agree that the violin was returned to Maria Robinson, Wallace Hartley's fiancée. She kept it for another twenty-seven years, and it then passed to her sister upon Maria's own death in 1939. After that, the violin's ownership is not completely known until 2006, when the son of an amateur musician unearthed it in the attic of her home. After seven years of testing, the violin was authenticated and presented to the Lancashire Titanic Museum. It was authenticated in part by the engraving of Maria Robinson's name on the silver stave. It was still housed in the leather valise bearing Wallace Hartley's initials.

# W. H. H.

Violin photographs copyright © 2019 by Tim Ireland—PA Images/Getty Images

WALLACE HARTLEY